LITTLE MISS SUNSHINE
and the Wicked Witch

Roger Hargreaves

Original concept by Roger Hargreaves
Written and illustrated by Adam Hargreaves

MR.MEN   **LITTLE MISS**

MR. MEN and LITTLE MISS ™ & © THOIP (a Chorion Company)

PSS!
PRICE STERN SLOAN

ISBN 978-0-8431-2490-3   10 9 8 7 6 5 4

Little Miss Sunshine was going for a walk.
The weather was not very nice, but it takes a
lot more than a bit of rain to dampen Little Miss
Sunshine's spirits.

In the distance, she saw Little Miss Bossy
approaching.

"I will be nice to Little Miss Bossy," thought Little
Miss Sunshine, "so she won't boss me around."

However, as she got closer, the most incredible thing happened. There was a bright flash and Little Miss Bossy turned into a bat!

A blue, very squeaky, bossy sort of a bat.

"How extraordinary!" exclaimed Little Miss Sunshine as she watched Little Miss Bossy flap her wings and fly away.

But almost as extraordinary was the cackling laugh Little Miss Sunshine thought she heard coming from the clouds above.

The next day was much nicer. The sun was out and there was not a cloud in sight. Little Miss Sunshine was happily walking along, wondering what had happened to Little Miss Bossy, when she saw Mr. Rude walking toward her.

"I will be nice to Mr. Rude," thought Little Miss Sunshine, "or he will be rude to me."

But at that moment there was a bright flash. And when Little Miss Sunshine reached where Mr. Rude had been standing, she discovered that he had turned into a toad.

A red, very rude, angry-looking toad.

And just like the day before, Little Miss Sunshine heard a cackling laugh. But this time it seemed to be coming from a nearby tree.

On her walk the following day, Little Miss Sunshine had nearly caught up with Little Miss Ditzy when there was another blinding flash.

Little Miss Ditzy had turned into a mouse!

A very confused, ditzy, blond-haired mouse.

When Little Miss Sunshine heard the same laugh she had heard the two days before, she ducked behind a bush and waited to see if she could find out who it came from.

Suddenly, with a rustle of leaves, a witch flew out from behind a tree.

A wicked witch on a broomstick!

A horrible, hook-nosed, hairy, warty wicked witch, dressed in black.

Little Miss Sunshine felt very afraid, but she bravely decided to follow the wicked witch into Whispering Wood. It didn't take Little Miss Sunshine long to find the wicked witch's ramshackle cottage.

Nervously, Little Miss Sunshine crept up to the window and cautiously peered in.

The wicked witch was standing beside a large black cauldron hanging over a fire. She was muttering to herself as she stirred revolting ingredients into the steaming pot. Little Miss Sunshine listened hard to hear what she was saying.

And this is what she heard:

"Hubble, bubble,
Toil and trouble,
Eye of newt and hair of hog,
Early tomorrow morning,
Turn Little Miss Sunshine into a dog!"

Little Miss Sunshine realized that she needed
help and she needed it fast.

She tiptoed around to the front door where the wicked witch had left her broomstick leaning against the wall. And without thinking whether she could fly a broomstick or not, Little Miss Sunshine hopped on.

As it turned out, she could. Just about. The broomstick rose up into the air with a wobbly Little Miss Sunshine perched on top.

Little Miss Sunshine knew exactly who would be able to help—Little Miss Magic. The broomstick took her to Little Miss Magic's house in no time at all.

"There's a wicked witch living in Whispering Wood," explained Little Miss Sunshine breathlessly when she arrived. She then told Little Miss Magic what she had seen and, more importantly, what she had heard.

". . . and I'm going to be turned into a dog tomorrow morning!" she gasped.

"That's awful!" said Little Miss Magic. "But this is just the sort of problem that I like dealing with."

"I hoped you would say that," said Little Miss Sunshine.

"Now, I'll tell you what we are going to do . . ." continued Little Miss Magic.

The next day, at sunrise, Little Miss Sunshine and Little Miss Magic knocked at the wicked witch's door.

The wicked witch opened it and with a flash, her spell turned Little Miss Sunshine into a dog.

"Hee, hee, hee," cackled the wicked witch. "That worked like a dream."

It was then that Little Miss Magic turned the wicked witch into a cat!

A smelly, scraggly black cat.

A smelly, scraggly black cat that suddenly found herself looking up at a scary yellow dog.

The wicked witch cat let out a screech and fled.

And, barking noisily, the Little Miss Sunshine dog set off in pursuit and chased the wicked witch cat far away. So far away that she would never find her way back.

When Little Miss Sunshine returned, Little Miss Magic turned her back into her old self. She then found Little Miss Bossy and Mr. Rude and turned them back to normal as well.

Little Miss Ditzy took a lot longer to find as she was hidden in a mouse hole, and being the ditzy person that she is, she seemed not to have noticed that anything had happened.

"Are you feeling all right?" asked Little Miss Sunshine after Little Miss Magic had said a few magic words.

"Why, of course I am," said Little Miss Ditzy. "Why shouldn't I?"

"Oh, no reason," said Little Miss Sunshine, winking at Little Miss Magic.

"Although," said Little Miss Ditzy, twitching her nose, "I really fancy a nice piece of . . ."